# CHICKEN SOUP for LITTLE SOULS READER

# The Greatest Gift of All

Story by
Lisa McCourt

Illustrated by
Tim Ladwig

*Based on the story "The Braids Girl" also by Lisa McCourt*

SCHOLASTIC INC.

New York   Toronto   London   Auckland   Sydney
Mexico City   New Delhi   Hong Kong   Buenos Aires

*For Karen Baliff, my ever-awesome Little Souls partner,*
*and for all the other amazing people at HCI*
—L.M.

*For Makayla*
—T.L.

*For Christopher, for truly understanding the meaning of selfless giving*
—J.C.

*This book is dedicated to inspiring you to be the greatest giver in the world*
—M.V.H.

*For my wife, Anne, and our children, Melinda and Hayley*
—P.V.

*For my daughter, Mandy, and my sons, Oliver and Robert,*
*in the hope this will inspire them to open and turn the pages*
*of this precious volume*
—G.S.

ISBN 0-439-69365-9

12 11 10 9 8 7 6 5 4 3 2 1     4 5 6 7 8 9/0

Printed in the U.S.A.     08

First Scholastic printing, September 2004

# CONTENTS

## CHAPTER 1
## MAD!

I was mad. And when I'm really, really, mad, the only person I can talk to is Grandpa Mike.

So I called him on the phone.

"Hi," I said grumpily when Grandpa Mike answered.

"Izzy?" he asked.

"Yes," I said, just as grumpily.

I waited for Grandpa Mike to start making me feel better.

"Rough day?" he guessed.

"Rough! You have no idea!" I shouted. "Summer is almost here, and EVERYONE — I mean EVERYONE — is going to Pine View Camp. Am I going to Pine View Camp? No! I am not going! Mom and Dad want me to go to Hilltown Community Camp. And NO ONE — I mean NO ONE — goes to that camp!" I took a breath.

"Hmmm. That *does* sound like a rough day," said Grandpa Mike. "Your parents are pretty nice folks. Why do you think they'd make such a horrible suggestion?"

"You know why!" I yelled. "Because it doesn't cost any money to go to Hilltown. That's all they care about! Money!"

Grandpa Mike gave a low whistle. "But, Izzy, you've known for weeks you couldn't go to that expensive camp. Why are you so upset today?"

"Because my best friend, Marisol, didn't keep her promise! She told me that if I couldn't go to Pine View, she wouldn't go, either. She said she would tell her parents that she wanted to go to Hilltown with me. She promised she would." I had to stop talking because I was starting to cry a little.

"So Marisol has decided to go to Pine View with everyone else?"

A big lump was stuck in my throat. I nodded my head, even though I knew Grandpa Mike couldn't see me nodding over the phone. I couldn't talk because of that big lump. It was the worst day ever.

## CHAPTER 2
# GIVE-BACK TIME

That weekend, Mom tried to cheer me up.

"When Dad starts his new job, it will be better," Mom promised. "We'll be able to do more of the things you want to do."

"Uh-huh," I said.

"Maybe you can even go to Pine View *next* summer," said Mom, brushing my hair out of my eyes.

"Okay," I said. I didn't tell her that next summer didn't matter. All that mattered was *this* summer. All that mattered was going to camp with my friends.

"I hear they do a lot of crafts projects at Hilltown," Mom said. "That sounds like fun. You love making crafts. And you'll get to ride a bus there!"

"Yeah, great," I said without meaning it.

Then I said something I shouldn't have said. "I hate it that my family doesn't have as much money as my friends' families."

Mom looked sad. I wished I hadn't said it. But that was what gave her the idea.

"Izzy," she said, "you know how Grandpa Mike does his Give-back Time on Sundays?"

Grandpa Mike had been doing Give-back Time for as long as I could remember. But I never really knew what it was. "Yeah," I said.

"How would you like to go with him tomorrow?" asked Mom.

I'd go anywhere with Grandpa Mike. Grandpa Mike could cheer me up no matter how terrible I felt. He was just like that.

So the next day, Grandpa Mike picked me up on his way to do his Give-back Time.

"Where do you do this Give-back stuff?" I asked him.

"Oh, you can find ways to give back just about anywhere," he said. "But for a couple of months now, I've been doing it at the Family Togetherness Home."

"What's that?" I asked.

Grandpa Mike said, "It's a place where moms and dads and kids stay when they don't have any money or any place else to live."

Together we walked to the Family Togetherness Home. I felt a little uncomfortable when we got there. Some of the people wore strange clothes. They looked tired. It scared me a little to be around people who seemed so different from me.

But Grandpa Mike smiled and said hello to everyone as if they were old friends of his.

"We're here to help these folks, Izzy," he told me. "Today we're going to help by passing out the food."

Grandpa Mike talked with the people in charge of the volunteers. He introduced me. He told them I wanted to help out. I didn't remember saying that.

Those people sure seemed to like Grandpa Mike.

"Would Madame like another biscuit?" he asked a lady. He pretended to be a waiter in a fancy restaurant.

Everyone laughed.

I pulled on Grandpa Mike's sleeve. "What am I supposed to do?" I whispered.

He brought me over to the counter. A
volunteer was spooning out soup into bowls.
"Help Margaret here," he said. "Or just look
around. See if anyone needs anything."

I looked around.  I saw lots of people who
seemed as if they needed things.  But I didn't
see how I could help them.

A girl sat in the corner.  She looked about
my age.  Her clothes were old and stained.
Her hair hung in two long braids. They were
coming undone because they weren't fastened

on the ends. The girl was sitting with her knees pulled up against her chest. She rocked back and forth with a sad look on her face.

Grandpa Mike saw where I was looking. He handed me a bowl of soup. "Why don't you bring that fine young lady some of this fancy chowder?" he said. "It looks like she could use some cheering up."

I took the bowl. I walked slowly toward the girl. I didn't know what I should say to her. As I got closer to where she was sitting, I almost changed my mind and turned around. But it was too late.

"Hi!" she said.

"Uh, hi," I said back.

"You can eat your soup here by me!" she offered.

*Oh, no*, I thought. *She thinks I live here, too.*

"No! I . . . uh . . . brought this for you,"
I explained. I put the bowl of soup down in
front of her. I walked back to Grandpa Mike
as quickly as I could. I tried to look busy
serving people food. I wanted the girl to see
that I was one of the volunteers.

I looked back at her. She was rocking again
with that same sad look.

On the way home, Grandpa Mike said, "I like doing Give-back Time with you, Izzy. You can come with me whenever you want."

"Why are those people so poor?" I asked him.

"Sometimes people make bad choices. And sometimes they just have bad luck," he said. "But we're all God's children, just the same."

I knew why Mom had wanted me to go with Grandpa Mike to the Family Togetherness Home. She wanted me to see how lucky I was. I didn't have Pine View Camp. But I had plenty to eat. I had neat, clean clothes to wear. We had our own warm house to live in.

I sighed. I knew Mom was right. But I still wished I could go to Pine View.

## CHAPTER 3
### WORRIES

When I got home, I called my friend Marisol. I wanted to tell her all about my day at the Family Togetherness Home. But as soon as she picked up the phone, she started talking about Pine View Camp.

"Have your parents decided to let you go?" she asked.

"No. They said I will have fun at Hilltown Community Camp."

"Oh," answered Marisol. "Too bad, but

guess what? That new girl, Nicolette, is going to Pine View. She is so cool! I hope she is in my group at camp!"

I really wanted to change the subject. I asked Marisol if she could come over after school on Monday.

"Gee, I would love to," she said. "But Nicolette already asked me if I wanted to go to the mall with her."

"Okay, bye," I said as I hung up the phone.

Now I had plenty to worry about. I had to figure out a way to go to Pine View camp. I had to get my best friend back from Nicolette. But instead of working on my problems, I kept thinking about something else.

I kept thinking about that girl with the braids. Why couldn't I just forget about her?

I wondered why she had to live at the Family Togetherness Home. Did she have any other clothes to wear? Did she go to school? Did she ever watch TV? Had she ever been to a movie? To an amusement park? To a museum?

I called Grandpa Mike. "I want to do Give-back Time with you again," I told him.

"I'm pleased as punch," he said.

Then I got busy. I opened each of my drawers. I opened my closet. I made a pile of all of the clothes that I knew didn't fit me anymore. The Braids Girl was a little smaller than I was. I guessed the clothes that were a little too small for me would fit her just fine.

"Mom, is it okay for me to give some of my clothes to a girl I saw at the Family Togetherness Home?" I asked.

"Which clothes?" Mom wanted to know.

"Just the ones that don't fit me anymore,"
I told her.

"I think that's a wonderful idea," she said,
hugging me.

It was hard to give up some of my favorite
things, even if they were too short or too tight.
My purple high-tops were the hardest to give
up. They had beautiful rainbow-colored laces.
I loved those shoes. I tried them on one more
time. They squished my toes so bad I couldn't
walk. But they were the coolest shoes I'd ever
had.

"She's going to love these," I said to myself.

## CHAPTER 4
### THINGS

On Sunday, I showed Grandpa Mike the bag of clothes.

"That's the spirit!" he said.

When we got to the Family Togetherness Home, I found the Braids Girl leaning against a woman. I guessed the woman must be her mother.

I started toward them. But I stopped. I wasn't sure about the bag of clothes in my arms. Would she like the same kinds of clothes I like?

How would her mother feel about me giving her the clothes?

When the Braids Girl saw me, she smiled. She ran up to where I was standing. "You came back!" she said.

"I just wanted to give you these clothes," I said. I felt nervous. I handed her the bag.

The Braids Girl looked down. Her smile went away. "Thank you," she whispered.

I hurried over to the other volunteers.

I helped Grandpa Mike the rest of the morning. I saw the Braids Girl looking at me. But whenever she saw me look back, she turned away.

On the way home, I asked Grandpa Mike, "Why didn't the Braids Girl like the clothes I brought her?"

"Oh, I'm sure she liked them, Izzy," he said. "But maybe that isn't what she really needs most."

I thought about that for a few days.

*What she really needs are some things of her own*, I thought. I spent the rest of the week deciding which of my things I could bear to part with. I had some favorite books. I had read them so many times, I knew them by heart. Maybe those would cheer her up. Some of my stuffed animals had seen me through plenty of sad days. Maybe they would help the Braids Girl feel happier.

I picked up the orange puppy that Marisol and I had won together at the fair last summer. For a second, I thought I might cry. I crammed it into the bag of things I was giving to the Braids Girl. Then I took it out of the bag. I stuffed it into the bottom drawer of my dresser.

Soon I had a bag filled with toys and books. I hoped the Braids Girl would like everything. I put in a comb and some hair bands and barrettes so she could fasten her braids.

Grandpa Mike was happy that I wanted to keep doing Give-back Time with him. He said the other volunteers had told him how lucky he was to have such a caring and special granddaughter. That made me feel good inside. But why didn't the Braids Girl make me feel that way?

## CHAPTER 5
## SUSAN

The next Sunday, the Braids Girl skipped over
to me before I even had a chance to look for her.
"Do you want to play hopscotch?" she asked.
She pointed to a hopscotch board she had
scratched in the dirt just outside the doorway.

"Um . . . no," I said. "I wanted to give you
this stuff. I hope you like it."

The Braids Girl looked in the bag. She
sighed. "Thanks," she said without a smile.

I didn't know what to say. I walked back
to Grandpa Mike. Nothing I did ever made
the Braids Girl happy.

"Why the glum face, Iz?" Grandpa Mike asked.

"I just don't understand," I said. "Every
time I give anything to the Braids Girl, she

looks sadder than she did before. I want to make people happy and do Give-back Time like you. What am I doing wrong, Grandpa Mike?"

Grandpa Mike knelt down beside me. "Well, first tell me something, Izzy. Why is it that you call that child 'the Braids Girl'?" he asked.

"Because she always wears her hair in those unfastened braids," I said. "And I don't know her name."

Grandpa Mike rubbed his chin. "Best way I know of to find out a person's name is to ask her," he said. "Give-back Time doesn't have to be hard. In fact, when you're doing it right, it feels better than just about anything."

He gave my hand a squeeze. Then he went back to joking and laughing with the people he had come to serve.

I looked at the Braids Girl. She was wearing my outgrown yellow jumper. But she didn't look any happier than she had looked in her own worn-out clothes.

I watched her. I thought about what Grandpa Mike had said. Maybe things were not all that she needed. Maybe what she needed most couldn't be carried in a bag. I was scared. But I knew what I wanted to do. It was what I should have done all along.

"Hi," I said. "My name is Isabella. But most everyone calls me Izzy."

The Braids Girl looked up. I think she wasn't sure if she could trust me this time. Then she smiled a super-big smile.

"I'm Susan," she said.

*Susan,* I thought. *A real person with a real name.*

"Want to play hopscotch?" I asked her.

"Are you sure?" asked Susan. "You really want to?"

"C'mon!" I said.

After we played, Susan looked in the new bag I had brought her. "How come you keep giving me things?" she asked.

I didn't know what to tell her. At first, I had wanted to help her because she was poor. But now . . . "Because I want to be your friend," I blurted out.

Susan smiled at me. "That's what I was hoping since the first time I saw you," she said. I took out the comb, hair bands, and barrettes.

"I brought these for your hair," I said. Susan ran her fingers down her braids.

She pointed to the barrettes. "Maybe with those," she said, "my hair could be like yours."

"Sure it could," I said. "I'll show you." I unbraided Susan's hair and combed it out. It hung loose and bouncy down her back.

Then I used the barrettes to pull back each side, just like mine. Susan ran over to a shiny stew pot to see her reflection. She looked pretty. She smiled happily.

Susan surprised me with a soft hug. "You're the nicest girl I've ever met," she said.

After that, I came to see Susan every week.

She was really easy to talk to. And funny. And smart. And we liked a lot of the same things, like horses and puppies!

One time I asked her, "So, why do you live here?"

"We moved into the Family Togetherness Home right before you started coming," she said. "My mom's job is to keep people's houses nice and clean. She cooks for them, too. And does their laundry. We were living in the house where she worked. But my mom lost her job, so we came here. We're only staying until she finds another job."

Susan's problems seemed much bigger than mine. But she was still a great listener. I told her all about Marisol and Nicolette. I told her about camp. Susan had left her best friends at her old school. I knew she didn't have many friends at her new school yet. But she never complained. And every time I saw Susan, she was wearing my old sneakers with the colored laces. That made me feel great.

## CHAPTER 6
# THE NEWS

School was almost out for the summer.
I was glad because school had gotten lonely.
Marisol still talked to me sometimes. But she
didn't have very much time to spend with me.
She was always with Nicolette. Who could
blame her? She and Nicolette had a whole
amazing summer to plan.

I really looked forward to seeing Susan on
the weekends. Then she told me the news.

Grandpa Mike and I had just stepped
through the door of the Family Togetherness
Home. Susan had been waiting for us. She

ran to me and grabbed my hands.

"Guess what!" Susan sang, dancing me in a circle. "My mom got another housekeeping job! We're moving out of here!"

I was a little surprised that Susan was so excited about that. I thought she liked it at the Family Togetherness Home.

I wanted to be happy for Susan. And I *was* happy for her. But at the same time, I felt bad for me. Would I ever see my friend again?

"Wow," I managed to say. "When are you moving?"

"Tomorrow," said Susan, jumping up and down.

I didn't know what to do. I knew I should say something like "That's wonderful!" But all that came out of my mouth was "I'll miss you."

Susan laughed. "No you won't!" she said. "Because we're moving into a house in Hilltown! And just in time for summer! I'll get to go to Hilltown Community Camp!"

I couldn't believe it. Susan at Hilltown Community Camp? I never thought I would see her outside the Family Togetherness Home. But she was a regular kid, just like me and my friends. And she wanted me to see her that way. That was all she had really wanted, right from the start.

"Awesome!" I said. And I really meant it.

Susan and I had more fun that day than ever. And I knew my summer would be perfect now, all because of her.

When it was time to go, I said good-bye to Susan. "I'll save you a seat on the bus on the first day of camp," I promised her.

"Wait," she said. "I have something to give *you* this time." She reached into her pocket. She pulled out a colorful braided friendship bracelet.

Susan took my arm and tied the bracelet around my wrist. The beautiful colors of the braided string looked familiar. A braided gift from the Braids Girl. Only she would never be just the Braids Girl to me again.

"That's so you'll remember me," she whispered.

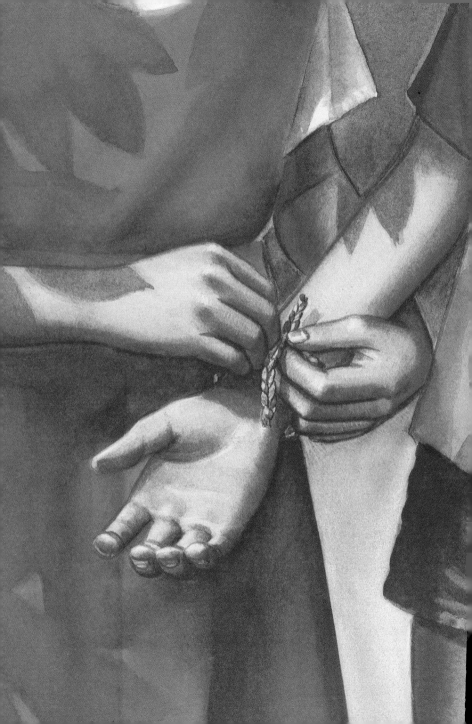

I suddenly knew why the bright colors in the bracelet looked so familiar to me. I looked down at Susan's feet. Sure enough, she was wearing my wonderful, outgrown, purple high-tops. Except they weren't nearly as wonderful now. The rainbow laces were gone. The shoes were held together by old gray-white strings.

All Susan had in the world were the things I had given her. And she had given up the prettiest of those things so she could make a gift for me.

Happy tears stung my eyes. "I'll remember you, Susan," I said. "I'll remember you for sure."